A LITTLE SUGAR
IN THE TANK

The editorial staff of *Miracle Monocle* is pleased to reveal the fifth volume of its micro-anthology series. This ongoing, innovative publishing initiative employs digital publishing techniques to address under-served communities in the literary world. Our hope is to offer worthy voices a new platform for expression and to illuminate under-served territories for our readers, while leveraging tools and resources from the UofL Writing, Editing, and Publishing Lab.

A LITTLE SUGAR IN THE TANK

miraclemonocle

Miracle Monocle
Louisville, Kentucky

First Printing: 2026

ISBN-13: 978-1-7341233-4-0

Miracle Monocle
University of Louisville
Bingham Humanities 315
2216 S. 1st Street
Louisville, KY 40292
miraclemonocle.com

Ordering Information: Copies of this book are available via the *Miracle Monocle* website and other online vendors. Special discounts are available on quantity purchases by corporations, associations, educators, and others. For details, please contact the publisher at the above listed address.

U.S. trade bookstores and wholesalers: Please contact *Miracle Monocle* at the above listed address.

Editor's Note

This book was conceived by the editorial staff of *Miracle Monocle*, an award-winning literary journal housed at the University of Louisville. The manuscript was produced as a PubLab initiative. All efforts were made possible by the generous support of the University of Louisville, the College of Arts and Sciences, the Department of English, the Creative Writing Program, and generous donors like you.

This anthology would not have been possible without the hard work and creative energies of our student editors, who are celebrated on our masthead. We welcome readers to share their thoughts about this book on our website: miraclemonocle.com

We'd like to thank all of the writers who shared their words with us; we have striven to do your work justice with this book.

Warmly,

Dr. Sarah Anne Strickley
Faculty Editor of *Miracle Monocle*
Founder of PubLab

Miracle Monocle

Miracle Monocle is an online journal of innovative literary and visual art. Published bi-annually, the journal features poems, short stories, literary nonfiction, and a broad range of experimental works. The journal is staffed by a team of graduate and undergraduate editors who earn course credit for assisting in the production of our issues. A faculty editor guides the editorial process, and creative writing faculty consult on the growth of the journal. Previously unpublished and emerging writers are highly encouraged to submit. Please visit our archives to sample issues of the journal and read our submission guidelines. Information about supporting *Miracle Monocle* is also available online. Donations are tax deductible to the extent allowed by the law.

Visit *Miracle Monocle* online here:
Website: miraclemonocle.com
Bluesky: @miraclemonocle
Facebook: @miraclemonocle
Instagram: @miraclemonocle
X: @miracle_monocle

Donate to *Miracle Monocle* and PubLab by visiting the "Support Us" tab on the *Miracle Monocle* website.

Table of Contents

A Dramatic Gesture

Blair Brienza

You were the civil war strategist
I the scruffy battalion drummer
       how did we meet?
It ends with your attempts to
divert my squadron away from
action while, a forest away,
I stride into the fire
better dead than apart.

You went to Hot Rabbit the night
I djed, I went up for air after
my set, you at the bar
melted me on sight so I sidled
up to the piano made up
songs to a stranger.

We were best friends skipped
gym together to rediscover
anatomy in the boys locker room.

We were angels made to face
forward but our eyes kept
slipping to each other and
suddenly our orders had funny
meanings. I giggled in God's
face once, when you shot me
that look.

You needed open heart surgery
and I was the only qualified
surgeon on the clock. Taken all
the way away away by your skin
I opened it, closed it back up.
I checked in on you early:

still groggy from the meds
you flirted with me.

My stoner friend Vaughn had
family friends in town and
drove me over to meet y'all.
Your mother sensitive like mine,
you a wildcat seething
under your smile like me.

We went to the park, sat
and played Beck and shared
earphones, glanced at each
other. Was this deja vu?

Tom and Huck sailed down
the Mississip, dirty feet
on their little boat
went ashore at Saint Louis
Memphis New Orleans
looked for trouble or work
and a hay loft to curl around
each other at night.

Caught on Film
Willie Edward Taylor Carver Jr.

The funny thing about college is that it's a liberatory experience, but it has an end date.

We rarely associate liberation with finite borders; our collective vision is of some expanding abstract that loosens edges, that plows over hurdles, that opens. But I took my final exam on a very specific day in May of 2006. I walked the stage to graduation weeks later, my family whooping, clapping, and yelling my name from the highest bleachers in the college gym as I took from a nameless university administrator a piece of rolled up paper that symbolized the end of my undergraduate experience.

They tore that gym down three years ago.

But I still have my diploma.

My first years of college felt like the academic Wild West with tiled floors and wooden desks. Professors talked about Appalachian liberation, about gender inequality, about race, class, and religion, and they wrote words like *gay* and *trans* on the board while we seriously considered the homoeroticism in poems by Emily Dickinson, the love-thought of bell hooks, the amorous freedom of Oscar Wilde cut loose in the streets of New York, and the deep-rooted sexual spirituality of Walt Whitman, who dared to love men and write about it. Outside of class, we marched on the State Capitol, we practiced and performed the *Vagina Monologues* and scandalous plays like *For Whom the Southern Belle Tolls*, and we desperately loved each other—and everyone in charge of my safety and education, for the first time in my life, said to me over and over again that the queer side of me mattered, that it had value, that it was welcome exactly as it was.

Every semester, the abstract became more complex. Every year, the abstract became more real.

I, too, became more complex, became more real.

But *real* in the context of my education classes was something different from the classes in primary content. Over time, my French courses became more subjunctive, my English courses became more intellectualized and speculative, my sociology classes more swept up in the nuanced theory undergirding our constructed realities. Real, then, was about seeing what lay underneath, to expose the atoms of our stories and our languages so we might begin to know what the world was made of. But in my education classes, those Freshmen and Sophomore courses in theory, history and philosophy toppled over into upper-level courses about *the profession*. Bulletin boards, the changing legal landscape, and which sports to learn so we might get hired became the focus of our work. Understanding *why* and *how*, it seemed, were questions left to researchers and philosophers. Teachers, it seemed, would only ever need to deal with the *who* and the *what*.

I don't blame the professors. They were right. We don't live in a country in which teachers are asked—or welcomed—to take part in the work *about* their work. Teaching is overwhelmingly done by women, and America does not care what women think. America only cares about what they do.

So I became a teacher.

I made the bulletin boards.

I built the lesson plans.

I made the blueprint of specification for the standards-derived summative assessment and aligned it to objectives that mirrored what the state required me to teach at the level at which the state required me to teach it.

My senior year, we finally put into practice the rules and regulations we had learned in the Teacher Education Program. We were to create a digital portfolio that we could send ahead to would-be future employers, one that showed off our teaching philosophy, our ability to build units and lessons, our vast knowledge of transient education bureaucracy, and, finally, a five-minute video of us teaching.

We were getting ready for the real world.

I asked a professor if I might teach a short lesson in an introductory French class. I dressed the part: I ironed my khakis. I wore dark socks. I put on a polo bearing our school colors—one that had been hiding in the bottom of my dresser drawer since I was handed it as part of orientation—and I went to the classroom with a new Expo marker in my pocket, ready to be a teacher, in some ways for the first official time in my life.

There were twenty-five first-year undergraduate students in the classroom, their desks facing the clean whiteboard. I found that I wasn't nervous at all because I knew the material—I loved the material—and I was excited to share it with them. They were learning the verb *pouvoir*—French for *to be able to*—and I knew the verb well.

An assistant from the Education Department set up the camera, I breezed to the front of the classroom, and I laid out the board into a conjugation chart, dividing the verb by number and person into its six present forms as I pronounced each carefully and flawlessly, emphasizing the rounded schwa-like vowel *œ* as a native speaker would, drawing on the students' knowledge of earlier forms to help them along, demonstrating patterns in vocalization to clarify every question that time would bring to them about the verb. In five short minutes, I had taught phonetics, historical linguistics, comparative grammar, sociology, had scaffolded psychology and developmental cognition, and had made sure that a couple dozen people, unable to only minutes before, could now confidently say *I can*.

The room flooded with affirmation.

Afterward, I headed to the computer lab and began my write up while a professor uploaded and sent me my video. It came within an hour, and, attached to it was a simple and honest note:

Willie,

This moment of teaching is truly breathtaking. You really know your content, and, more importantly, you know how to connect with students. Still—and please understand my intentions here—the truth is that your voice, your gestures, and the way you hold your hands comes across as fairly gay.

I just thought I'd tell you in case you wanted to redo the filming. I wouldn't want it to hold you back or keep you from getting a job.

I wish I could say that it hurt or that I was outraged. It didn't and I wasn't. I sat in a computer lab in a regional university in the middle of eastern Kentucky and all of my training—in English, in language, in sociology—showed me a world that I already knew, a world outside of the comfort and safety of my liberal university, a world that was not free.

I thought for a second about deleting the video and refilming.
Then I opened it.
I watched.

5

And yes, I saw my unabashed gayness in the softness of my voice and the flamboyance of my hands. But I also saw students excitedly copying the board, saw them raising their hands, watched them taking in a new concept, saw their worlds opening up and becoming bigger and newer and more possible, and finally heard a chorus of young Appalachians repeating over and over again in a foreign tongue *je peux, tu peux, il peut*. I can. You can. He can.

I downloaded the video to my hard-drive, and I felt Oscar Wilde directing the mouse, felt Emily Dickinson attach the file, felt Walt Whitman type my name at the top.

But it was me who hit submit, and a rush of freedom began to chip away at the walls.

Bodies Above the Tides

Coriander Focus

Her/men/u/tics

Kale Hensley

Bear with me—I really tried, really!
　　　　I practiced divinity in the so underwhelming
tenor of masculinity, but it had no hold
　　　　on my mansion of sloppy axe swings. Listen,
what work can a woman do condoned
　　　　to corners while all the fucking is happening?
I guess brother Joseph is here with me.
　　　　Now, don't confess you missed the passages
where the Holy Spirit is proudly a she!
　　　　The Mother Mary and her lesbian love-child
are laughing. How embarrassing—but
　　　　it makes the most sense, doesn't it? The boys
of Pentecost begged our otherworldly
　　　　lady to lay it on thick; bless the army, useful,
finally! Oh, how gallantly they tumbled
　　　　out windows to the hound-happy. I can still
smell it. Not Jesus' bloody lips. Jezebel's
　　　　ghost sitting below having a peaceful smoke.
I promise! The whole book is like this.
　　　　It'll do you some good to sit down. Read it.

The Gay Lunch Table

T.S. Leonard

before PrEP, but just, and after the world
wide web made it easy to catch strange men
in small places, we have so much terrible sex:
my first time; the dog guy; that set designer;

      etc.   ASL? bi dl   pnp   neg ddf
      we relearn the alphabet. We make up the rules
      at our all boys Catholic school lunch table: me,
      William, Hunter, Max—our shared language;

lol   omg   *Missouri loves company*
we search in private mode, incognito
window, scrubbing history and the next day
we debrief about what depravity we have seen:

      str8 bttm   raw 3some   gay4pay
      Will & Grace, Project Runway. We plan our escapes:
      Hunter first: to Paris. William, New York. We sneak out
      to catch *Brokeback Mountain* on the big screen. We learn

HTML   AIM   mp3   WMV
and how to download illegally. We watch bareback scenes
in a bathroom stall at choir. We march against war but not
for gay marriage; too easy to get caught. We read by flashlight

      books on AIDS, ACT UP, DOMA, from the LGBT section
      at the library. We hang out there and an all-night diner where
      you can still smoke inside. We fill red ash trays, playing grown;
      a waiter winks: *a boy like you shouldn't leave his cream behind*;

strip mall hotel, suburban house, empty parking lot.
We lie and say we are nineteen because that sounds more
believable. We lie and say we haven't done this before. Lying
back, they say *this was fun*. We turn eighteen. We keep going;

a guy renting someone's damp attic room tells me how
all his friends from high school had died: *the 90s*, he said, *was a different time*.
I don't know what to do so I hold him
and he sings "I'm On Fire," softly, to me or someone gone,

in the dark. Illegally, I download the song, put it on a CD—
soundtrack to our last summer driving around. Borrowed
memory, how it comes back louder through speakers;
how it changes. By the time we start spreading out

to AUP and NYU and me, to the middle of Missouri,
I start to notice a shift. In the rearview, I still catch it;
how lucky we were to survive all of that. How lucky
we were to survive all of that together.

Offering

Andrew Mack

The grave plots are mine:
an inheritance,
now that the family
has been hauled off,
dead,
to be buried at
some other church.

The sound
of this empty
graveyard:
howling
catbirds nearby
with splayed beaks,
hunting mates.
Beauty to them
is an open mouth.

Remember:
Back then, stopping at graveyards
along the way
to church
each Sunday,
we identify kin;
the way a birdwatcher
identifies birds
by their beaks
the pallor of their feathers,
their songs.

Mother asks:
How we can
believe in God if we
cannot see

him?
and I reply,
So much of the world
is an open mouth
we cannot see.
Mother, rock steady
even in those last days,
does not flinch,
only turns herself
toward the window;
Close your mouth, she says,
hold your breath
when you pass
the graves.

The Sunday sermon:
followed by a
hog roast, the pig
first scalded,
then impaled to roast
over a spit, the mouth
held open by a steel bar
rotating above hickory coals
and fed by deacons and
congregants.

We see:
grease drips
over the
flames, smoke stings
the eyes.
Nearby graves
watch carefully
while the congregation
opens their mouths,
prays,
devours.

Gay

Madari Pendas

Adjective.
1. "Bright, lively."
2. "Keenly alive and exuberant: having or inducing high spirits."
3. "Given to social pleasures." Also: LICENTIOUS.
4. "Of, relating to, or characterized by sexual or romantic attraction to people of one's same sex."

Gay

Noun.
5. "Sometimes disparaging + offensive; see usage paragraph below: a gay person especially a gay man."

–Merriam-Webster Dictionary

(1)
The cafeteria
is bright & lively
with the vim & vigor
of children.
We sing & shout,
imitating the macaws
we saw hovering over
the live oak,
pomegranate-red plumage,
brilliant, honorable,
we all tried to call it
to our forearms,
as if we could
command or control
nature.

I hear the word
first as an insult,
in the cafeteria,
breaking through the din,

three tables down,
lunch almost over.
I look for the mouth,
but everyone's chewing
& talking & Kate C.
is asking me about a sleepover.

You're so gay!

I hear it again,
I swivel out of my seat,
to find the voice.
I don't see the speaker
but the receiver:
Mike R.
His head is set
over his crossed arms.
His flat pizza & tater tots
uneaten, cooling.
I know this face,
I know any face
on the verge of wailing.

(2)
Mike & I
used to chase
iguanas until
they skittered
up the sabal palm,
disappearing
into the green scrub.

We felt exuberantly
& brilliantly alive,
dashing toward
a group of lounging
lizards, their red

dewlaps flashing,
warning us to stay away,
until they bolted
into the cavern
of a gutter.

Were we drawn to one
another,
able to sense
the jitteriness
of the other's secret?

(3)

When summers
reached 105 degrees,
Mike & I retreated inside,
afraid that we'd literally
melt—we had watched
the *Wizard of Oz* together,
each aping the Witch's death,
flat on our bellies,
puddled ladies.

We wrote notes
to people in our class
on construction paper,
trying to make smooth-edged
hearts with pink safety scissors.
They were invitations
to a fancy tea party;
we'd even get real,
non-caffeinated jasmine tea.
I'd wear a top hat.
Mike said he'd borrow his mom's
slick, thick pearls.
It'd be splendid,
splendid;
Puddled ladies.

18

(4)
I don't know why I
thought this, but
as we entered high school
it felt like being gay
was somehow worse
for boys.

Boys seemed
riotous, louder,
a thick tangle
of muscles & hair
& fists.

We, girls, were
allowed
to sleep close to one another,
to even practice slipping
our tongues into one
another's mouths.
And still be straight.
Mike disappeared first year,
transferred,
transformed,
maybe it was too much.
He had been caught
in the student parking lot
behind a Tercel,
knees graveled.
Licentious.

(5)
In the elementary cafeteria
the other boys
finish off his food,
flinging some torn
tato bits at his head,
a scrap smacks his lip,

then rolls down his philtrum,
then chin.

He looks down,
already defeated—
for some reason,
I think if he had called
the macaw over
it would have come to him.

Excerpt from "THE ECSTASY OF SAINT SEBASTIAN"

Eric Robert Shoemaker

Saint Sebastian was buried outside the walls of Rome—
the stone walls of Aurelius, Diocletian's predecessor.

> If you found his lonely body
> cast into the sewer,
>
> caked in dry blood and shattered by so many cudgels and bashers,
> would you pick him up?

People say most conservatives only understand
how *human* queers are
when one of their family
becomes queer to them.

What is it, a start?
Pretty pitiful, a canned response:
sorry you're
afflicted
wrong
I'm Christian so I have to love you, too.

> Sebastian's body would be so riddled with holes,
> would be so splintered,
>
> he wouldn't look like your son.

The priest said
he's not different;
he's your same son,
You just know a little more about him now.
I was so grateful at the time,
grateful for that haunted start.

I am haunted by all priests and priestliness
and the vague anxiety of trespass I can't recall.
The altar boy robe-room
haunted by a different predator every five years,
a revolving door of assholes,
a tar pit inescapable—
each man sticks a hand in and
grips the glop,
each boy-ghost struggles for air
and sinks in the brown shit
and dies
a very slow suffocation, paralyzed,
fighting, punching, clawing out
with shame in their ears leaking into their young but now so much older mind
Haunted.

Only the one priest even tried
so many others bit
and gripped
so many others hid in the tar
and pitched wings over wounds
to fly-hop like turkeys
while carrying goslings in talons
to harpy in twisted trees with broken boys

   Sebastian's body is vulnerable and soft.
   He's beautiful, but sad.

   You want to cheer him up,
   but your impulse is for you.

   Would you pick up
   every body on the street—
   corner or gutter—
   every sad, hungry eye
   every thirsty sadness
   every drink/too little

    every shot/a lacerated bullethole
    everybody/deserted

They say St. Irene nursed Sebastian
back to health; the arrows didn't
kill him enough. They say she fed,
watered, clothed him. They say she
protected him until he could rise.

They say Sebastian found Emperor Diocletian, and now, fully healed
and clothed, resurrected and
as triumphant as that boy
could ever be again after beating
and shooting,
his rapturous, angelic body holy,
Sebastian defined his own victory,
determined on what terms
he would march into death.

Diocletian was amazed.

They say Sebastian
was then left in the sewer
and discovered by a holy widow
who buried him outside the Aurelian walls.

And sure, that shell was buried.

We all leave something behind
for others to mourn and puzzle over.

(I think he ascended
(I think he was assumed

(I think Sebastian broke his chains
(I think Sebastian flew by and by
(I think his body was just part of the story

(I think his story is importantly incomplete

(I think,

(Between you and me,

(He is smiling

There Are Two Brides

Cassandra Whitaker

There are two kisses   before wishes shared become a new name
For one The other retains   the name—the house—the land—the sires
The name There are two   names One before One after

Names One I chose   In choosing I entered a new name
A new country growing   from myself—yet inside myself
There are two brides   one and one in which one resides

There are two brides?   There are too many deaths to name
Here The brides   —inside DNA—tell stories—I cannot be the only one
Straying from lines   so invisible that even when seen there is no vision

There are too many joys   to name To name them is to engender them
An engine for joy has parts   One part is a new name Another part is friends
A big part is laughter   A wedding is a celebration that runs on joy's engine

A bit of food—a bit of drink   The dancing's stomping will keep away the night
As long a love shares   as long as love shares There are two brides
There are two kisses   before wishes shared become a new name

Pain does not find   Booze—the strap—the back of hand
A famine's famine   the kind of love that fleshes flesh A wolf's love
There are two brides   There are two grooms There are wives' wives

Contributors' Notes

BLAIR BRIENZA (they/them, he/him) is a mid-sized tiger in a temporal jungle. He comes from Chickasaw land, their heart lies in Wandownock, and his feet are on Ayyulshun. @blairbrienza

WILLIE EDWARD TAYLOR CARVER JR. is a minoritized youth advocate, Kentucky Teacher of the Year, and the author of *Gay Poems for Red States*, a Stonewall, American Library Association, Read Appalachia, Whippoorwill, and Book Riot-award winning collection shortlisted for 2024 Judy Gaines-Young Book Award. His novel, *Tore All to Pieces*, will be published in 2026 by the University Press of KY. Willie's writing has been published in *Appalachian Journal, Southern Humanities Review, Young Ravens Review, Another Chicago, Harbor Review, Smoky Blue Literary, Miracle Monocle, Good River Review, Salvation South*, and *Gay & Lesbian Review*. Willie believes everyone deserves to feel that they matter.

CORIANDER FOCUS is a full time creator, working most in the mediums of multimedia photography and written word. Focus spent her youth deep in the mountains of rural Appalachia where her love of wild places was cultivated; out of that passion came original art and poetry inspired by the natural world and its influence on our internal experience. Focus explores work that tells a story about how we relate to ourselves and our bodies using photography, poetry, and multimedia art that frolics through the forest. She has worked as an artist and has had her work displayed nationally across galleries, shows and publications since 2010. Notable highlights of Focus' recent career have been Peter Bullough Foundation - Summer AIRS (2025) Her Voice, Her Vision - Chesapeake Arts Center (2024) Windows to the Inside - Woman Made Gallery (2023).

KALE HENSLEY is a poet and visual artist from West Virginia. Her work appears in *BOOTH, Evergreen Review*, and *Gulf Coast*. She lives in Texas with her wife and a menagerie of clingy pets. Find more of her writing at kalehens.com

T.S. LEONARD is a disco poet time machine from Kansas City, Missouri who lives and teaches in San Francisco. Leonard's poems have appeared in

Poetry, Foglifter, and *fourteen poems*. His debut collection, *Another Anthem of Fabulous Survival*, selected by Meg Day for the 2024-2025 Poetic Justice Institute Prize, will be published by Fordham University Press in 2026.

ANDREW MACK is the Founder and Managing Editor of Loblolly Press, a publishing house dedicated to uplifting emerging and marginalized voices from the American South. He is the author of three poetry collections: *Weekend Revival, What the River Was*, and *Beasts of Chase*. He lives in Asheville, NC, with his partner.

MADARI PENDAS is a writer, poet, painter, and cartoonist. Her work has appeared in *Craft, The Columbia Journal, The Masters Review, The Maine Review*, and more. She is the author of *Crossing the Hyphen* (2021) and *She Loves me, She Loves me Not* (2025).

ROBERT ERIC SHOEMAKER is the author of *Magical Poetics* (Bloomsbury Academic, forthcoming), *Ca'Venezia* (2021, Partial Press), *We Knew No Mortality* (2018, Acta Publications), and *30 Days Dry* (2015, Thought Collection Publishing), and he is the translator of *Catherine of Siena: Prayers* (One Subject Press, forthcoming). Eric earned a PhD from the University of Louisville. Follow him at reshoemaker.com

CASSANDRA WHITAKER (she/they) is a trans writer and educator who lives in rural Virginia. A member of the National Book Critics Circle, Whitaker's work has been published in *Michigan Quarterly Review, Conjunctions, The Mississippi Review, Gulf Coast, Foglifter, Lambda Literary Review* and other places. *Wolf Devouring A Wolf Devouring A Wolf* is out from Jackleg Press in July 2025. Visit wolfs-den.page to learn more.

Miracle Monocle thanks you for the purchase of this book. We hope that you enjoyed it and will support future titles released in conjunction our new publishing initiative: *The* Miracle Monocle *Micro-Anthology Series.* All proceeds from the sale of this book will go toward the realization of future titles in this series. Founded in 2009 as an annual digital literary journal, *Miracle Monocle* is now an AWP-award-winning biannual journal, as well as a training program for students with ambitions in the field of publishing, and a nexus of literary programming in Louisville, Kentucky. We pride ourselves on serving as a home for innovative literary art that might otherwise go unnoticed in a crowded media landscape; we are also committed to showcasing writers who might regularly escape the attention of traditional or commercial publishers. We take pleasure in juxtaposing emerging talent with established voices. For readers interested in learning more about *Miracle Monocle,* or writers who might be interested in joining the ranks of our contributors, we invite you to visit us online.